DRACULA

Bram Stoker

NOW AGE BOOKS
ILLUSTRATED

PENDULUM PRESS, INC., WEST HAVEN, CONNECTICUT 06516

ISBN 0-88301-093-3 Complete Set
         0-88301-100-X This Volume

Library of Congress Catalog Card Number 73-75460

Published by
Pendulum Press, Inc.
The Academic Building
Saw Mill Road
West Haven, Connecticut 06516

Printed in the United States of America

TO THE TEACHER

Pendulum Press is proud to offer the NOW AGE ILLUSTRATED Series to schools throughout the country. This completely new series has been prepared by the finest artists and illustrators from around the world. The script adaptations have been prepared by professional writers and revised by qualified reading consultants.

Implicit in the development of the Series are several assumptions. Within the limits of propriety, anything a child reads and/or wants to read is *per se* an educational tool. Educators have long recognized this and have clamored for materials that incorporate this premise. The sustained popularity of the illustrated format, for example, has been documented, but it has not been fully utilized for educational purposes. Out of this realization, the NOW AGE ILLUSTRATED Series evolved.

In the actual reading process, the illustrated panel encourages and supports the student's desire to read printed words. The combination of words and picture helps the student to a greater understanding of the subject; and understanding, that comes from reading, creates the desire for more reading.

The final assumption is that reading as an end in itself is self-defeating. Children are motivated to read material that satisfies their quest for knowledge and understanding of their world. In this series, they are exposed to some of the greatest stories, authors, and characters in the English language. The Series will stimulate their desire to read the original edition when their reading skills are sufficiently developed. More importantly, reading books in the NOW AGE ILLUSTRATED Series will help students establish a mental "pegboard" of information — images, names, and concepts — to which they are exposed. Let's assume, for example, that a child sees a television commercial which features Huck Finn in some way. If he has read the NOW AGE Huck Finn, the TV reference has meaning for him which gives the child a surge of satisfaction and accomplishment.

After using the NOW AGE ILLUSTRATED editions, we know that you will share our enthusiasm about the series and its concept.

—The Editors

ABOUT THE AUTHOR

According to the Reverend Montague Summers (an authority on vampirism and author of *The Vampire: His Kith and Kin* and *The Vampire in Europe*), the vampire is "one who has led a life of more than ordinary immorality and unbridled wickedness; a man of foul, gross, and selfish passions, of evil ambitions, delighting in cruelty and blood." Bram Stoker creates such a man in the character of Count Dracula.

Stoker was born in Dublin in 1847, at a time when reports of vampirism were rampant. He made the most of these in his tale of horror, *Dracula*. The story is enhanced by the superstitious nature of the people, and the protective measures they take to escape vampires. Garlic and crucifixes become especially significant as they save the life of the intended victim more than once in the story.

In addition to *Dracula*, certainly his most famous contribution, Stoker also wrote dramatic criticism and articles for the *Dublin Mail*. One story, *Dracula's Guest*, was to have been the opening chapter to *Dracula*, but the story survives well without it. He wrote one other novel, *The Lair of the White Worm*, but it is little known.

Bram Stoker
DRACULA

Adapted by
NAUNERLE FARR

Illustrated by
NESTOR REDONDO

a
VINCENT FAGO
production

Jonathan
Harker

Mina

Lucy

Count Dracula

Dr. Van Helsing

From Jonathan Harker's Diary. . . .

I had come here on business, but what I found has scared me beyond belief. I am locked in. The only way out is through the windows. These may be my last words. This castle is my prison but I must escape and warn the people of London about Count Dracula.

NESTOR REDONDO

GOLDEN KRONE INN

It was a long trip on which my business company sent me from the busy London of the 1890s to the wild Carpathian Mountains of Transylvania. On May 31, I reached Bistritz, last stop before Castle Dracula.

Are you the Englishman?

Yes, I am Jonathan Harker.

Welcome! Count Dracula has told us how to help you.

A seat had been saved for me on the Bukovina coach leaving the next morning, but at the last minute, the innkeepers tried to keep me from leaving.

But it is St. George's Eve!

At midnight the dead rise; evil has full power! Wait a day!

When I told them that my business could not be put off, the good woman made me wear her cross.

Wear it. . . for your mother's sake!

I had read that every known superstition in the world comes from the Carpathian Mountains.

I must have fallen asleep and dreamed. . .for the trip was like a nightmare. The carriage seemed surrounded by howling wolves. . . the horses were scared. Then the driver got down, waved his arm, and the wolves turned around and ran. I must have dreamed! A man cannot control wolves.

Suddenly there were rattling chains and the clanking of large locks. . . .

Count Dracula!

Enter freely and of your own will!

I am Dracula! Welcome to my house! Come freely. Go safely; and leave something of the happiness you bring!

His grip is as strong as steel and as cold as ice!

Come in! You must be chilled and hungry!

The fire and food were welcome sights and did away with my fears.

Come, your bedroom is ready. Sleep as late as you wish tomorrow . . . I must be away.

Sleep well and dream well!

Thank you, Count.

So began my stay at Castle Dracula. I thought strange things, but was too tired to know what was real and what I only dreamed.

The next day I found a cold breakfast waiting for me.

Strange. . . everything is ready, but no servant.

In the room next to the dining room I found a library with a good English section, even including railway guides and local maps!

But all day, I saw no one. . . heard nothing but the wolves outside. The castle seemed empty.

The Count returned and again dinner was served. But still no servant, and Dracula did not eat anything.

Afterward we talked about Carfax Abbey, the property bought for Dracula in London.

I am glad that it is old and big. To live in a new house would kill me.

The chapel is here.

I am happy that there is an old chapel. We Draculas do not like our bones to lie with the common dead. We are a proud and old people.

The blood of Attila* flows in my veins. We Draculas have defeated many people. We are proud and love war. You might say we are bloodthirsty.

But come, my friend, write to your employer and say that you shall stay with me for a month!

You wish me to stay so long?

I will not take no for an answer! Did not Hawkins say that you would follow my wishes?

* A German chief who helped destroy the Roman Empire.

What could I do but stay? I was there on business for Mr. Hawkins, not on my own.

The days passed. I looked through many rooms of the castle. . . .

But I saw no living person. . . .

. . . .and always came to a locked door. There was no exit!

Another strange thing was that I could find no mirrors in the castle.

It's a good thing I brought my own shaving mirror.

One evening Dracula came up behind me without my hearing.

Good evening, friend Harker.

Count Dracula!

. . . .and also unseen.

But. . .I can't see him in the mirror!

I frightened you. . .you've cut yourself!

Suddenly the Count's eyes filled with fury and he grabbed my throat!

There is blood on your throat!

But, sir. . . it is nothing. . . .

A cross!

At sight of the landlady's gift, Dracula's strange fury passed.

Be careful how you cut yourself. It is dangerous in this country!

It is this terrible thing that has caused the cut. Away with it!

Count Dracula. . .no!

Time passed in this lonely nighttime way of living. Keeping my diary was one of the things I did.

Is the Count a madman or am I? Practically I am his prisoner, with no way out and no communication with the outside world. Perhaps soon when a month is up, he will send me safely on my way...

And my mirror shattered into a thousand pieces on the rocks far below.

Often, I stood at the open window of my prison, breathing fresh air and looking over the countryside. Then one night. . . .

Something is climbing on the wall!

It is Dracula. . . climbing down the wall!

I went to bed with fear in my heart. What manner of man is this. . .or what manner of beast that looks like a man?

I slept, then suddenly awoke. There was bright moonlight. . . and a feeling that I was not alone! I lay still unable to move.

It will make me feel better to have the old lady's cross nearby.

Go on! You are first and I shall follow.

He is young and strong; there is blood enough for all.

As if under a magic spell I could not move. I watched these strange women come closer from under my eyelids.

My throat! If only I could reach the cross!

Suddenly as if from nowhere. . . .

How dare you touch him when I had told you not to! Back! This man belongs to me!

But are we to have nothing?

Good he sleeps.

I promise you shall have him when I am done with him tomorrow.

Horror overcame me and I passed out. When I opened my eyes again, it was daylight and I was alone.

When the people back in the village spoke of Vlkoshak. . .vampires . . .I thought they were superstitious and ignorant. God help me, I was the one who was ignorant. Now I know the Count wants me to die today.

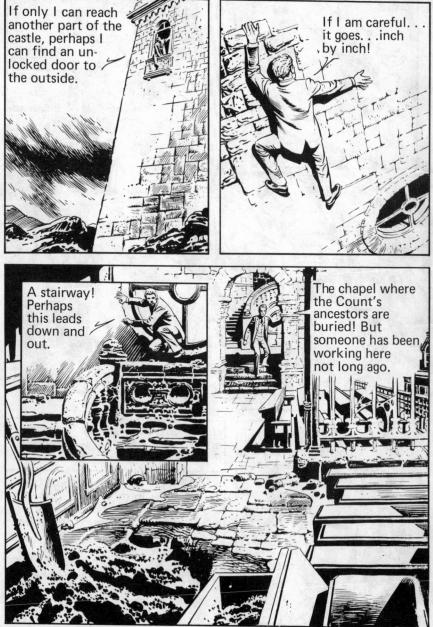

I was without hope. Anything was better than sitting and waiting for death.

If only I can reach another part of the castle, perhaps I can find an unlocked door to the outside.

I remembered the sound of the mirror smashing on the rocks, and was careful not to look down!

If I am careful. . . it goes. . .inch by inch!

A stairway! Perhaps this leads down and out.

The chapel where the Count's ancestors are buried! But someone has been working here not long ago.

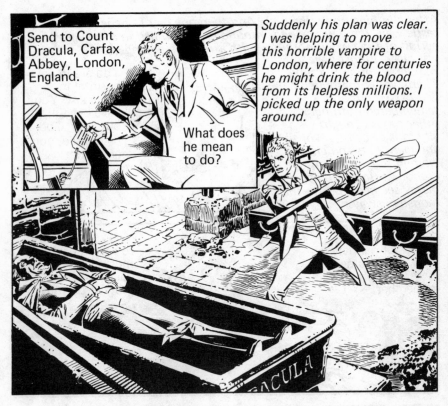

Send to Count Dracula, Carfax Abbey, London, England.

What does he mean to do?

Suddenly his plan was clear. I was helping to move this horrible vampire to London, where for centuries he might drink the blood from its helpless millions. I picked up the only weapon around.

But a person can't kill the Undead with just a shovel! Though he was asleep, the Count's eyes seemed to stop me and the shovel dropped from my hands.

I. . .I cannot strike!

There was no way out of the chapel but the way I had come in. There was no escape down the wall, death was better than staying as Dracula's prisoner.

I must take my chances. . .and pray that it is not too far down.

After climbing down the castle wall, there was a long period of time when nothing was clear. I must have wandered for a long time. There were times when I just passed out and remembered nothing. At other times I fought with all kinds of beasts. Wolves and giant bats and ghost women fought for my blood. At times, an angel of mercy seemed to drive the monsters away.

And then one day I opened my eyes and found myself in bed in a strange room, with a nurse standing nearby.

Where am I?

You are in a hospital in Budapest. You have been ill, but now, God be praised, you are better!

I felt very weak and mixed up.

Sir, what happened? How did I come here? I can't remember.

You must not try to remember! You must relax and keep calm and grow strong again.

I was surprised to learn that I had been ill for nearly six weeks! I knew that my friends and Mr. Hawkins must be worried and the nurse wrote to them at once.

To Miss Mina Murray, and to Mr. Peter Hawkins.

We were worried that we did not know how to let your friends know sooner.

Mina came to me as quickly as boat and train could bring her, and it was a happy day when we were together again.

Mina!

Jonathan! My dearest!

Years later Mina told me of the warning that the doctor gave her.

He has had a very bad shock which caused brain fever. Be careful that nothing else like this excites him for a long time to come. He will probably be weak for a long time.

This warning made her ready to agree to my wishes about my diary.

I don't know whether the things written here are real or the ideas of a madman. I can't remember them, I don't want to read them, but I have a feeling it should not be destroyed. Will you keep it?

I will put it away, and hope we never will need to look at it again!

We were married almost at once by the English minister. It was not the wedding we had planned, but still a beautiful and happy event!

I now pronounce you man and wife!

It was still a few weeks before I could leave the hospital and return to England. To fill my mind, Mina told me of what had happened to her while I was away.

I had visited the seaside town of Whitby myself, and I could picture the two girls there.

You've often heard me speak of my dear friend Lucy Westenra. Lucy and her mother were vacationing in Whitby and invited me to join them there. It's such a lovely place.

The first day we walked around the village and found what became our favorite spot.

"We sat there often," Mina said, "and talked of you and Lucy's fiance, Arthur Holmwood."

We had one problem. Lucy began to walk in her sleep. She hadn't done that since she was a child.

Lucy, dear. . . .

Lucy's mother asked me to lock our bedroom door at night and keep the key.

Her father did the same thing! I am so afraid she will have an accident, and hurt herself.

She's excited about her coming wedding, and she misses Arthur!

One night there was a terrible storm — nobody slept!

That ship!

It will crash on the rocks!

The Daily Graph

GREATEST AND MOST SUDDE STORM ON RECORD STRIKES WHITBY HARBOR

Miraculous Escape of Vessel

But the ship did not land on the rocks. Instead it was found on the sandy beach. At the moment it hit. . . .

The safe landing seemed even more strange when it was learned that it was steered by the hand of a dead man!

Look! A great dog!

More like a wolf.

Dead! And for days, I'd say!

And not another person on board!

The Captain's log, read at the investigation, told the story of a terrible voyage!

July 6—Finished taking in cargo, silver sand, and boxes of earth. Ship Demeter, sailed from Carna at noon. Crew, five men. . .two officers and myself (Capt.)

July 16—Mate reported one of the crew, Petrofsky, missing. Could not explain it. Crew upset.

July 24—Entering Bay of Biscay, last night another man lost. Took crew and searched ship. Found nothing among cargo of stacked coffin-like boxes.

We've searched from stem to stern, and there's no one else aboard.

July 29—Second mate is missing and crew is afraid. They believe there is an evil person aboard.

It is here. He is here! Save me! Save me!

July 30—Last night we slept soundly. Awakened by mate telling me that both man of watch and steersman missing. Only self and mate are left!

August 1—Had hoped to land somewhere to port, but we are surrounded by a mysterious fog. Mate seems to be going mad.

August 3—Still fog. Running before wind as mate and I could not handle sails alone. At midnight mate ran to me on deck — a raging madman.

DEMETER

Before I could move to grab him, the mate threw himself into the sea.

Stop, man!

The sea will save me from him. It is all that is left.

I have seen him and the mate is right. But I am captain and must not leave my ship.

I am growing weak. I shall tie my hands to the wheel and hold this cross. He will not dare touch it!

Weeks had passed while Mina told me what had happened. At first she could visit me only a short time each day. But I got better quickly—soon I could walk to the balcony and sit in the sun.

The outcome of the investigation was an open one. . .the mystery could not be solved. But to the Whitby folk, the poor Captain who brought his ship and cargo safe to port, was a hero!

And the dog?

The dog disappeared into the darkness and was never seen again. . .though many people looked for it and wanted to help it.

Strange. . . .

But Mina, at that time, was having more important problems; my long absence was still a mystery, and Lucy was sleepwalking.

Lucy? She isn't here, and the door key is gone!

Her clothes are all here. She didn't dress. She can't have gone far!

Quietly I looked through the house but could not find her. . . and the outside door was open! I threw on a robe and rushed out.

There was not a soul in sight. I ran along the walk but could see no sign of the white figure I looked for.

She'll be chilled, I'll take a wrap. But where can she be?

Could she possibly have gone to our favorite seat? I don't know where else to look!

Yes, she is there! And there is someone or something. . . behind her!

I ran as hard as I could, and I called out.

Not a soul in sight. . .and Lucy is still asleep!

She was breathing in long, heavy breaths, and her throat seemed to hurt her.

Poor dear, she must be chilled.

I tied the blanket at her throat with a safety-pin to leave my hand free, and gently awoke her and led her home.

Oh, Mina! Where am I? What did I do?

Sssh! We'll soon be home, dear.

The next morning when we awoke, Lucy seemed well, but I was worried when I saw two tiny red marks like pinpricks on her throat.

Oh, Lucy, your throat! How clumsy . . .I must have stuck you with the pin last night.

It's nothing at all. I can't even feel it!

The next morning, Lucy was pale and without energy. But a letter in the morning mail lifted her spirits.

It's from Arthur. He is coming here. He wants us to be married at once.

I am so happy for you, my dear!

But at that time I was even more interested in my own letters.

News from Jonathan at last! Oh! He has been ill. He is in Budapest. Mr. Hawkins will send me to him at once.

And so Mina's story of our being apart had a happy ending, with our marriage and my return to health; and we left the hospital and Budapest with thanks to the kind people there.

Good-bye, and all my thanks!

I hope I can care for him as well as you have done.

Good luck and all happiness.

God bless you both!

As the train neared London, I was happy to be there. I had been away a long time.

Almost home! Mr. Hawkins wrote that he would meet us with his carriage.

I am eager to hear about Lucy and her wedding plans.

After dinner, Mr. Hawkins had a surprise for us.

My dears, your health and success! I've known you both from childhood. Now I want you to make your home here with me. I am all alone, and in my will I have left you everything!

It was a happy evening. We could hardly offer our thanks. But perhaps, Mr. Hawkins had had a warning. For three nights later he died suddenly in his sleep! It was a shocking blow!

Let us pray for our dear departed friend.

To help us forget we walked home from the funeral. Suddenly on the crowded street. . . .

My God! It is the man himself! Do you see?

No dear. I don't know him!

I felt ill. . .dizzy and shaken. I might have fallen if Mina had not helped me to a nearby bench.

I believe it is the Count, but he has grown young. My God, if this is true! If I only knew!

Oh, my dear, you are ill again! I'll call a cab and take you home.

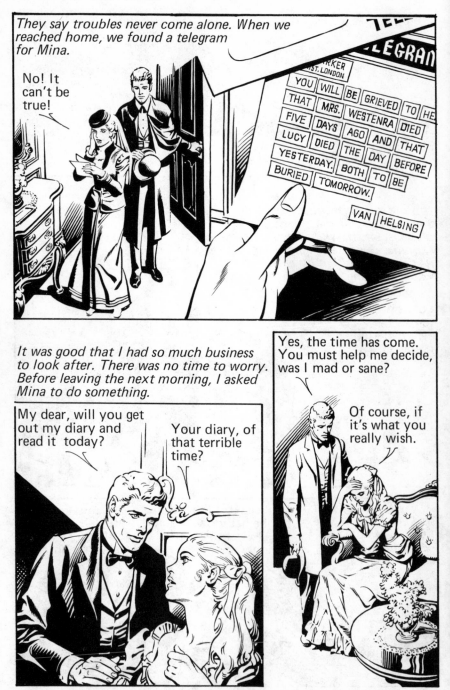

They say troubles never come alone. When we reached home, we found a telegram for Mina.

No! It can't be true!

YOU WILL BE GRIEVED TO HE... THAT MRS. WESTENRA DIED FIVE DAYS AGO AND THAT LUCY DIED THE DAY BEFORE YESTERDAY. BOTH TO BE BURIED TOMORROW.

VAN HELSING

It was good that I had so much business to look after. There was no time to worry. Before leaving the next morning, I asked Mina to do something.

My dear, will you get out my diary and read it today?

Your diary, of that terrible time?

Yes, the time has come. You must help me decide, was I mad or sane?

Of course, if it's what you really wish.

Poor Jonathan! Was it brain fever, or is what he writes true?

These things seem connected. That fearful Count was coming to London and Jonathan was so sure he saw him yesterday!

If only there were someone we could ask for help! But who would believe that Jonathan was not mad?

At that very moment, an important letter arrived for Mina.

From the foreign doctor who took care of Lucy. He has read my letters to her and knows of our troubles. He wants to see me!

It's like an answer to a prayer! I'll ask him to come tonight. He is worried about what happened to Lucy, but still he might help us.

So when I returned home that evening, I found we had an important visitor.

Dr. Van Helsing, this is my husband, Jonathan.

Happy to meet you!

How do you do, sir?

And so we heard the sad, strange story of Lucy Westenra's sickness and death.

When Dr. Seward could not cure Miss Lucy's illness, he sent for me to come from Amsterdam.

I am so weak. Sometimes I can hardly breathe, and when I sleep, I have terrible dreams.

Don't worry, my dear. We will take care of you!

I agree there has been much blood lost, but she is not anemic*. Yet there must be a cause! I must go back home and think!

* an illness that affects the blood

For two days there were good reports from Dr. Seward to Amsterdam; then on the third day, a telegram arrived.

TERRIBLE CHANGE FOR THE WORSE. COME AT ONCE.
SEWARD

When Van Helsing saw Lucy again, he was shocked at her unnatural paleness.

She will die in need of blood! There must be a blood transfusion at once.

I have sent for her fiance.

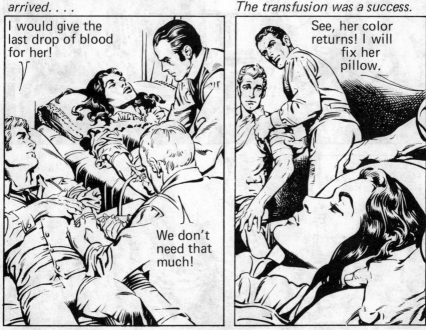

As soon as Arthur Holmwood arrived. . . .

I would give the last drop of blood for her!

We don't need that much!

The transfusion was a success.

See, her color returns! I will fix her pillow.

After another blood transfusion Lucy got her strength back.

Enough! She will be fine now.

See what I brought for you, Miss Lucy, all the way from Holland!

Oh, flowers!

You are teasing me! These flowers are only garlic*.

It is no joke! Garlic is a medicine which will be good for you.

How funny, like a magic spell to keep out evil spirits.

Exactly like that!

* a plant used to flavor foods and sometimes as a medicine

Do not take the flowers off your neck—and do not open the window tonight!

I promise. And thank you for all you've done!

During the night, Lucy was awakened by a loud howl from outside.

What is it? I'm frightened!

I was uneasy about you, darling. Are you all right?

You'll catch cold, Mother. Lie down beside me.

Suddenly there was a crash and a thin gray head came through the glass.

A wolf! Heaven help us!

It's all right, Mother, the garlic has stopped it!

My mother pulled at my flowers.

Mother dead, the maids asleep, the wolf still howls outside. God help me to stay alive this night!

In the morning the doctors looked over the scene with sad white faces.

My God! Both dead?

Miss Lucy is still alive. Quick. . . another blood transfusion!

Shall I send for her fiance?

Yes, quickly. She will come to soon, but I fear death is near.

Lucy awoke, and told us of the awful night. Then she slept, and Arthur Holmwood arrived.

We will call you when she awakens, I promise.

Suddenly there was a strange change in Lucy's face.

But her teeth are sharper. . .her eyes look wild! And the throat marks have gone!

Holmwood came in, and Lucy called to him in a new, exciting voice.

Arthur, my love, kiss me!

Lucy, darling!

Van Helsing grabbed Holmwood and pulled him away; Lucy's arms fell and eyes closed.

Do not go near her for the safety of your soul and hers.

As Lucy died, the terrible look left her face. Her face once more showed its own pure beauty.

It is the end.

Not so. It is only the beginning!

What do you mean?

We must save Miss Lucy from the life of the walking Dead! You and I, Seward, must perform an autopsy*.

We must remove the head and the heart from the body.

No! Never! I won't have her cut apart!

Good God, man! We loved her! Don't you understand?

I understand. You do not. But I hope there is still time to change your minds.

* an operation done to find out why a person died.

Mina and I were upset by Dr. Van Helsing's story.

Oh, poor Lucy!

But even on my way here tonight I learned that there is no more time.

Has something else happened?

Did you see the story of the small children who were missing from their homes overnight?

The ones who said they were tempted by a "Bloofer Lady"? Yes. . . .

But they were not hurt.

Each child who spoke of a "Bloofer Lady" had two tiny throat wounds—just over the jugular vein*!

Throat wounds — like Lucy's.

At Castle Dracula, it was always the throat those monsters went after.

* a major vein in the neck

And so my friends, I come to you for help.

Of course — anything!

But what can we do?

I need Miss Mina's story of Lucy's sleepwalking — and the diary of your visit to Castle Dracula!

Van Helsing left with the diary, saying we would hear from him soon. We waited nervously.

But his letter came the next day, and the news was good.

He swears that I am not mad and never was mad!

He says that you are sane — and also strong and brave!

But if the diary is true. . . is Dracula really in London?

Van Helsing asks us to come and stay at Dr. Seward's tonight. Perhaps he will explain everything then.

When we reached Dr. Seward's house that night, I made a surprising discovery.

Carfax Abbey. . .the place I bought for Dracula. . . it is next to Seward's.

Quick, we must tell Van Helsing!

But Van Helsing, Seward, and Holmwood had left to carry out an important mission.

While we waited, Van Helsing was leading the other men to a surprising place.

Dr. Seward asks that you make yourselves at home.

A graveyard!

For God's sake, where are you taking us?

Trust me! I must prove to you that things you don't believe are true!

The tomb where Lucy is buried!

Yes. Arthur will you open it with your key?

No! I forbid it! This is not holy. . . .

Van Helsing led the others outside to a hidden spot near the tomb.
A bell struck midnight. Far away, a dog howled.

Like a vampire, the Undead
Lucy fed upon the child.

At the sound Lucy pulled back
like a cat, with an angry growl.

When she saw Arthur, Lucy's
anger changed to a smile, her
voice to a devil-like sweetness.

Arthur, as if under a magic spell,
moved toward Lucy.

Her role as a vampire has just begun! These children whose blood she sucks are not yet bad, but if she continues, they will lose more blood and die.

They will then come under her power and become as she is. They attack others in a circle of evil which grows larger! But if she were to become a true dead. . . .

Yes, what then?

The children will get better. And the soul of this poor lady will be freed to take its place with the other angels!

She must be freed, Professor! But how?

A stick must be driven through her heart. Her head must be cut from her body and her mouth stuffed with wolfsbane*. I have brought the things we will need.

I will do it! It shall be my hand that sets her free!

Take the stick in your left hand, place the point over the heart and strike! Do not stop until it is done.

* a plant much like garlic

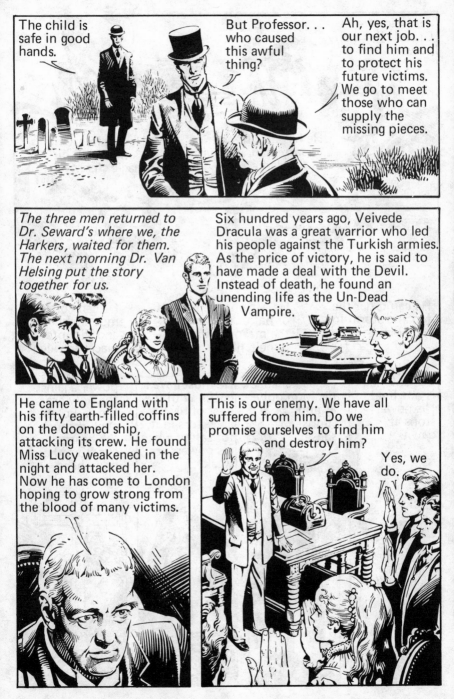

The child is safe in good hands.

But Professor... who caused this awful thing?

Ah, yes, that is our next job... to find him and to protect his future victims. We go to meet those who can supply the missing pieces.

The three men returned to Dr. Seward's where we, the Harkers, waited for them. The next morning Dr. Van Helsing put the story together for us.

Six hundred years ago, Veivede Dracula was a great warrior who led his people against the Turkish armies. As the price of victory, he is said to have made a deal with the Devil. Instead of death, he found an unending life as the Un-Dead Vampire.

He came to England with his fifty earth-filled coffins on the doomed ship, attacking its crew. He found Miss Lucy weakened in the night and attacked her. Now he has come to London hoping to grow strong from the blood of many victims.

This is our enemy. We have all suffered from him. Do we promise ourselves to find him and destroy him?

Yes, we do.

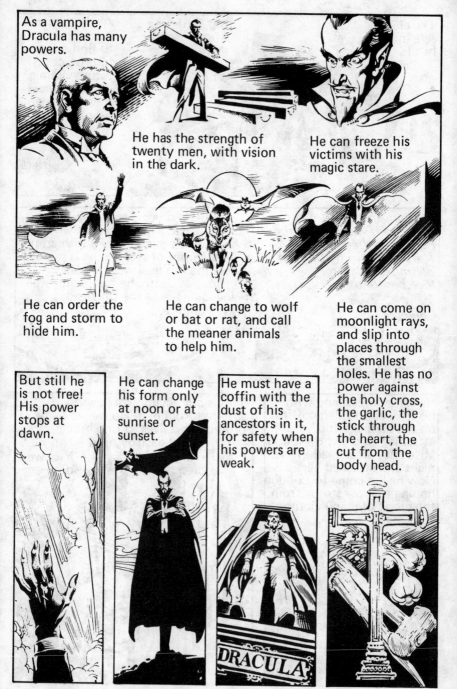

As a vampire, Dracula has many powers.

He has the strength of twenty men, with vision in the dark.

He can freeze his victims with his magic stare.

He can order the fog and storm to hide him.

He can change to wolf or bat or rat, and call the meaner animals to help him.

He can come on moonlight rays, and slip into places through the smallest holes. He has no power against the holy cross, the garlic, the stick through the heart, the cut from the body head.

But still he is not free! His power stops at dawn.

He can change his form only at noon or at sunrise or sunset.

He must have a coffin with the dust of his ancestors in it, for safety when his powers are weak.

DRACULA

In daylight hours, he must have a place to hide. If we can find his fifty coffins and make them unlivable to him, he is powerless. That is our first job.

I have the necessary information at my office.

Unnoticed Seward had walked to the window.

A great bat at the window! I can no longer stand the creatures.

Dracula himself, trying to over-hear our plans!

In a few hours I had done what I must and reported back to my friends at Dr. Seward's.

Fifty coffins were delivered to Carfax Abbey, but some were later removed.

Good work! Tomorrow we will find them. Now for a good night's sleep.

In our bedroom I fell asleep at once but Mina was restless and uneasy. Later she described what happened next.

Oh! What is it? Who's there?

The sun rose on a tired and worried group of people. But Mina was brave, and there was work to do.

We've destroyed the coffins stored in the Piccadilly House.

And we've taken care of those in Bermondsey.

Now, quick, to Carfax Abbey!

But when we returned, Mina met us with a heartbreaking story.

We broke into the old Chapel where the coffins were kept, and set to work.

For each a bunch of wolfsbane and a cross . . .and the vampire is kept from them forever.

Fifteen coffins destroyed in Piccadilly, and sixteen in Bermondsey. . . .

And eighteen here. There is one missing! Then Dracula still has a safe place! We've lost him!

There is still hope. Madame Mina can help. Let us return to her.

The evil marks are on my throat. I can feel Dracula's mind looking into mine, to learn your plans. Before I bring harm to you, I must die!

No, my child, you must not die. While Dracula is still among the Un-Dead your death would make you as he is! You must live. . . and help us.

It was a terrible journey. We travelled always by the fastest means, but Fate. . .or was it Dracula. . .slowed us down.

We missed
some trains.

Boat engines
broke down.

And our coach
lost a wheel!

But we always protected
Van Helsing's valuable
bag and our weapons.

I thought of Mina and with a great effort I fell on top of him, driving my knife into Dracula's throat as Holmwood drove his through the Vampire's heart.

For Mina!

For Lucy!

For all mankind.

It was like a miracle. Before our very eyes, the body crumbled into dust as the sun set.

At the instant Dracula's body crumbled to dust, the marks left Mina's throat. Van Helsing, the next day, entered the Castle to bring a merciful second death to the Un-Dead sisters there.

To a brave and daring woman and the men who did so much for her!

And so our terrible task ended where it began, at Castle Dracula. It was seven years ago. Our dear Van Helsing, who led us through the flames, is godfather to our son and shares our present happiness.

THE END

WORDS TO KNOW

ancestors	howling	vampire
bloodthirsty	ignorant	
chapel	superstition	

QUESTIONS

1. What were some of the things that happened at the castle which made Harker uneasy about Dracula?

2. Why did Dracula throw away the mirror?

3. Why did Dracula move to London?

4. Why didn't Harker destroy Dracula when he found him asleep in the coffin?

5. Why do you think Harker couldn't remember what had happened to him at Dracula's castle?

6. What happened to the men aboard the ship that brought Dracula to England?

7. What is a blood transfusion? What good was a blood transfusion after being attacked by Dracula?

8. What animals could Dracula change into?

9. How can a person protect himself from a vampire?

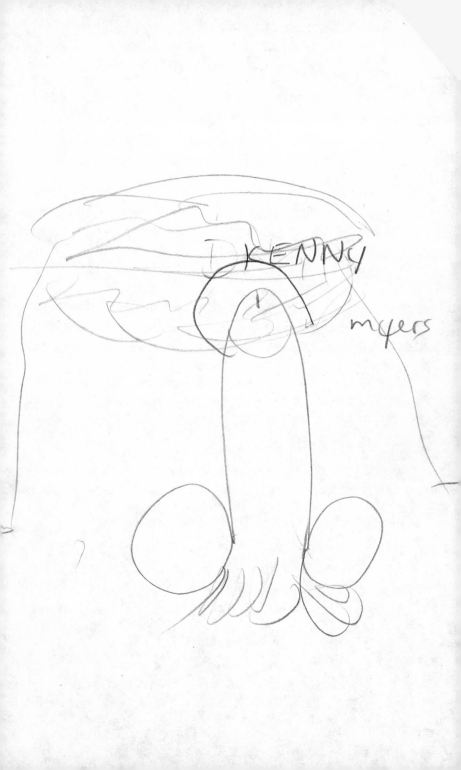